Murder on Christmas Eve

First Edition

Murder on Christmas Eve

VoroBooks, Etobicoke, Ontario, Canada

ISBN: 978-1-7383199-5-4

Typesetting and additional design by Lee Thompson Editing+

To contact the author: Nick_Voro@hotmail.com

MURDER ON CHRISTMAS EVE

ICHAEL WALKED OVER to the enormous bay window. He had a hankering to watch the sunset from inside this stereotypical mafioso mansion, which took its architectural cues from kingpins like Al Capone and his hideaways from federal agents and rival mafia families. The sun was slowly setting in the wintry distance. Spilling redness. Bloodying the surrounding snow-covered land canvas. Spreading that breath-taking crimson as more snow started to fall. One of those picturesque sights perfectly worthy of pictorial format.

He stiffened from a draft. A penetrating gust from an improperly installed window. Michael examined the time on his wristwatch, then left the poorly insulated window with its miniature mistral wind and walked over to the antique mahogany Victorian-era coffee table where he generously helped himself to a vodka eggnog infusion, sending his cup to the bottom of the bowl, a deep diving dunk until the sweetish alcoholic mixture reached the brim and overflowed, dampening his sleeve slightly in the process with the viscous alcoholic nectar inside.

A hearty sip followed from a swan-shaped mug while he fished in his pockets for a handkerchief. Once located, Michael wiped the dampened spot on his sleeve before he returned the now syrupy-sticky handkerchief back to that same pocket. With mug in hand, he walked back over to the picturesque sight at the bay window. The sun had now set. A storm raged somewhere close by. Within a minute the weather turned, significantly altering the landscape, intensifying everything outside, bringing along severe snow and treacherous conditions. Even the Japanese topiary gardens he admired earlier had now disappeared, everything fully entombed in white.

Michael gulped another mouthful of the cup's contents and walked deeper into the room, away from the window and its spectacular snow scene, his swan-shaped mug purposefully left behind, placed on the closed lid of a grand piano situated near the window, guaranteeing a water ring. He knew the water would seep in, staining the lid, the finish unsalvageable if not gotten to in time by the owner of this prestigious mansion; the owner unfortunately indisposed at this very crucial, potentially waterlogged-piano-lid type of moment. Oh yes, indisposed indeed, resting peacefully: a motionless corpse sprawled out near his killer's scuffed leather shoes.

A candy cane protruded from the corpse's left eyeball while a steady blood rivulet seeped out and stained the antique Persian carpet beneath the slowly cooling body. Michael nonchalantly looked down at the corpse. A killer admiring his handiwork.

Snow and more fucking snow. Christmas... a holiday everyone is supposed to like. And those who hate it quickly become outcasts. But I for one not only hate it, but everything that it represents. Just look at that fucking snow. I wish I were on the Cayman Islands right now instead of being stuck in a blizzard in this empty house. And thanks to this asshole, now just another exterminated loudmouth, I am stuck here for a good long while. Forgive me, dear reader, I am a bit cranky. Still adjusting to these newly prescribed anti-depressants, which supposedly help with stabilization of the mind. Side effects include: severe fucking with one's concentration. You should have seen what I did to the doctor who prescribed me these. Unfortunately, the writer of this story, as well as my life story, is lacking the masculinity to depict it as it actually happened. But just between the two of us while he's stepped out of the room, what he failed to jot down was the scene in the doctor's office, a great and gruesome bloody mess of a scene. It is almost ironic the publishing company would allow a description of a corpse with a candy cane sticking through the eye socket in all its graphic glory, but not this. Hypocrites. You see something wrong with this? Because I do. Anyway, back to this doctor prick and what I didn't do to him, but actually did. I broke every single one of his fingers. One for every time he used the word "depression," or any of its synonyms. And believe me when I say he used more than ten. It got to the point where I had to break his toes. But I let him off the hook after a while. The smell was sickening. The bastard pissed all over himself, his chair, and the floor. Now you might ask why I caved in and took the pills in the end. Well at first, I didn't see it the way he saw it, didn't agree with what he had to say. Now I have come around. I should probably send him a "I Hope You Feel Better Soon"

Hallmark card. They really did help with the mood swings, which I was getting more often than some dames I know. Sure, my concentration might be a bit off, but this might even out in time. For now, I'm giving the pills a try, following the doctor's advice. Since the writer is still not back, this would be the part where he'd tell you about how I gripped the corpse by the ankles, walked backwards and dragged it out of the room. The floor becoming instantly bloodied with, well... blood. The kitchen would replace the living room, a change of scenery for the cadaver. I would try to catch my breath, wiping my perspiration-covered forehead with the vodka eggnog-stained handkerchief. Don't ask me how come there is so much blood. Beats me where it's all coming from. I only poked him in the eye. I just know his maid isn't going to like this mess. Moving along... after this brief breather of catching my breath I would resume my hold on the body, open the door leading to the cellar and proceed to drag the corpse down into that cobwebbed catacomb. A dog, the owner's dog, would follow me closely behind.

Not that I noticed it until I reached the bottom, carelessly dropping the body. I would say something sadistically sarcastic like, "Weren't much help to your owner were you pal?" The dog would whimper a little. I would bend down, retrieve the bloodied candy cane from the corpse's eye and throw it to the dog. Another sadistically sarcastic remark from my lips along the lines of, "Here you go, mutt. Gourmet dog food courtesy of your more than generous owner." The dog would instantly devour it. And if you dear gullible fools think for one split second that he didn't know there was blood on that sugary peppermint treat representing Jesus' purity, you are in denial, folks. Will you look at me? Just look at me, ranting away. Rant to paper method of storytelling. Not good. Not good at all. But this is what happens, folks, when you have an absentee writer, barricading himself in his bathroom, over-analyzing the same descriptive sentence about a fucking sunset. So I am taking over. Getting one over on the writer while he tries so hard to find the perfect words, construct the perfect sentence, wanting to impress the literary

*hordes and give his entrusted Editor a headache
by repeating himself repeatedly, vomitus of verbal
tautology. He has no idea I am doing this internal
monologue, running amok, taking the reins of this
project. You must also be wondering when this slow
perfectionist is going to get to giving up a few details
about the dead guy now relocated to the cellar. You
need this information to find out exactly what you
should feel toward him, the dead guy. Should you
feel sorry since he is the victim and hate me for slay-
ing a good man? Or congratulate me for ridding the
world of a good-for-nothing son of a bitch? I hate
to be the bearer of bad news, but there are no good
guys in this story. Just criminals—various degrees
of deceitful, cunning, and despicable individuals.
But for your sake, I will help you out. Simplify the
matter. Help you root for someone. With this said,
you might as well root for me. (Pause) I am sorry
for the narrative pause; I just had an outburst of
seemingly pointless anger, kicking the corpse violently, enjoying the sound of his ribs breaking under
the force of my foot, then stopping as suddenly as I*

had started. It may seem pointless, but that couldn't be further from the truth. As soon as I begin to tell you my story, you'll see that my present actions are more than justified. First, let me tell you a bit about myself, and how I got tangled up with this asshole. Who am I? Just a simple narrow-minded criminal, or is there dimension and depth to me? Maybe I am just a cardboard cut-out. Let's give a breather to this narrative technique and find out. I'd rather show for once than tell. Keep in mind, I am no pretentious word scribbler who takes an infinity to jot down one fucking sentence, I get to the point I am trying to make. And if you find it violent, hurtful, and too realistic you can stop reading it, I won't be offended. This is real life.

A small apartment with hairline cracks along the walls and an unmistakable feeling of desolation. A pair of suitcases rest near the door. My former wife, I mean, *Michael's* current wife occupies the only chair sitting behind the only table. She is a knowledgeable woman, a woman of the world—intelligent, cultured, a person happy to oblige you if she cares enough about you. Her only problem is she is the type of woman you love for her mind and not for her sexual appeal, though she is charming. *Was this right? Did I do this correctly? I might need some practice.*

Michael walks through the door, instantly notices her.

"Where were you?" she says. "Answer me, dammit!"

He gestures with his hand for her to remain calm. "Don't raise your voice. There's no need to raise your voice."

She looks at him with plain disbelief. "No reason... no *reason*? You are out until the early hours of the night, and I shouldn't worry?"

"If I knew you were so worried, I would have called."

"God, you are pitiful. All you ever do is twist my words around until they lose all their meaning. Just a smart ass with his arsenal of smart-ass remarks. I am so sick of them. Of you. You used to be a writer. A writer, Michael. Now what are you?"

"I am still a writer." He smiles broadly.

"To call yourself a writer you actually need to write. You don't do that anymore. You hang around low-life sleazes, like that degenerate gambler Timothy Price, and you are becoming stupider. Just look at the words you use. Nothing but profanities."

"He is a friend."

"I am your friend! Your best friend. Your wife. And I am sick and tired of your goddamn stupidity. See what you made me do? Your foulness is rubbing off on me."

"Hey… come on… come here."

"Don't you dare. Tell me right now. Tell me what I want to know. Are you willing to change?"

"I don't know how you think I used to be; I am what I am now."

"Is that your runaround way of saying no?"

"You got it, toots. Now are you going to make dinner, or should I grab something from the corner deli?"

"No, Michael, I am not."

And there you have it. The beginning. Well… close enough. That was the last time I saw my wife. Her skittishness and nervousness, the way she took the room in for the last time, wringing her hands, strangling all life from them, running those same hands through her graying thinning hair… I hate that memory. I hate that it stuck around. Constantly reminding me of itself. Its existence lodged in my head. Replaying everything in slow motion. The way she stood up, walked over to the front door, took a suitcase in each hand, and left the premises. I remember I ran to the door, a last-ditch effort to hear her high heels out in the hallway. I forgot about the carpet. The carpet muffled all sound. So, I stood there like an idiot. Listening. All the while, she was long gone. Either this tale will help to humanize me a little or make me even more of an asshole than I already seem like. Killing a man and all. And will you just look at that dog, licking its chops from that candy cane. Hey, if you were here you might look on with perverse interest as well. Not something you see every day. I know I promised you to get to the matter at hand. The corpse on the floor. I just wanted to tell you something about the past, about me. When she left, it was what these shrinks call the "trigger effect" and no matter how bad I was before, I was worse after, and everything that happened from that day on, happened because of that day. I stopped living for a while. Then I started up again, but I wasn't the same, making bad decisions and amassing dangerous acquaintances. Spending all my time downtown with the drunks, prostitutes, and trash. The neon lights became my guideways. I mapped out the course from one bar to the next. One night in a drunken frenzy at a seedy watering hole where I was finishing the last glass of whisky I could legitimately pay for, a guy stumbled in, crazed, out of his mind, pulled out a gun and shot the place up. Talk about chaos and commotion.

Screams, bodies and blood everywhere, and just me and the sharply dressed gentleman next to me continuing to drink at the bar like nothing happened. He complimented me on my calmness and bought me another. I didn't know him. But I knew what he was. Once I accepted that drink it was too late. Sure, I saw the warning signs, but my life was over. I'd lost her, I was an aimless drifter, self destructive, looking for trouble. That man took me under his wing. Showed me the ropes. Introduced me to the trade. In no time I was doing odd jobs for the mob. Odd jobs soon turned into specific jobs. The sharply dressed gentleman then introduced me to The Boss. He was his right-hand man, and I was his. He trusted me. And that trust got me my first serious assignment. Surveillance. To tail The Boss's main squeeze, Alessandra, and, if caught in the act, to get rid of her and whoever she was seeing. I was the guy who handled things that needed handling. Old fashioned American boy with a passion for blackjack, disdain for the law and love of fast women. And this wasn't just any old job, this was

an opportunity for advancement—forget ripping
off easy marks, blasting and shoving off, this was
a high-class broad that came with a hefty price tag,
this would open doors. It always sounds easier
than it actually is. That's how they get to sell it to
you. I tailed her for a while, never much to report,
she was either innocent or too smart for me. I was
about to throw in the towel, pack up and go see The
Boss with my final report when she did something
different (if you call going inside a hotel different).
I followed her, tipped the miserable prick manning
the ship and got her room number. I couldn't believe
it. I had the jitters. I'd never murdered anyone
before. Undoubtedly, this was all about to change,
I had my instructions, and I didn't dare show up
empty-handed to the adultery party. I was packing
an unlicensed Beretta with a screwed-on silencer
and grip tape on the handle, a pair of black tactical
gloves on my hands. I reached the room and lock
picked my way inside. There she was. Stark naked.
Mounting some chump. They had no idea I was
there. Watching them. Moving. Moaning. When

they switched positions, that's when I pulled the trigger. Bang. A blood geyser. Cranial splattering. He coated the walls. The sheets. Her. She was so stunned she didn't even scream. She just pushed the dead man away, snatched a crumpled pack of cigarettes and a lighter from the nightstand and walked over to the chair near the bed, never caring that my gun followed her every movement. Alessandra then sat down, crossed her legs, and lit up a cigarette, looking me up and down. I should have shot her right then and there. Instead, I decided to open my mouth and ask her a question. A mistake that resulted in this mess here.

"Who's the guy?"

"A paying customer."

"Greedy."

"So, he finally decided to put a tail on me."

"He did."

"Took him a while. Almost had me convinced he trusted me."

"Evidently, not enough. Otherwise, I would

have never got the gig."

"Don't be naïve, you aren't the only one, they never send just one guy. No matter how good you are. Even the tail has a tail."

"So, if I don't kill you, they will kill me."

"That's the idea."

I speechlessly stared at her body like a prepubescent schoolboy. I couldn't help myself. I mean, what would you have done in my position? Face to face with a striking beauty, stripped and puffing seductively on her cigarette. I second guessed myself. And while I churned things over, she took a final, long drag on her cigarette, expelled the perfect smoke ring, uncrossed those runway model legs and lowered her blood-spattered hand.

"Don't…"

"I wonder what kind of lover you are. Hopefully not the selfish type. I've always believed pleasure should belong to all participants."

I don't know why I let her start, why I led her on instead of easing her pain and simply getting it over with. Maybe it was the power, a perverse pleasure in having so much control. I had her life in my hands, after all. Her hopes, her dreams, her fate... Look now, I knew she was an actress performing a role. Acting out her part. But as she dreamily brought herself to an orgasm, massaging herself in all the right areas, I still found it impossible to look away. I stood, stared, and noticed. I noticed her nails, filed to perfection. Her cunning, sensual mouth. I noticed her insane hunger for life. She was willing to do anything to stay alive. And there I was, a voyeur. A peeping tom peeking in on a private moment of sexual self pleasure. She moaned louder. I noticed her breathing increase, her hand movements become more vigorous; having reached the point of no return, she moved her hips forward, and arched her strong sweat covered body in that worn down chair, making me bear witness to an explosive climax the likes of which I'd never seen before. Explosive. That's the word. But I was soon over it. She came, and I came to my senses. Awoke from my spellbound trance. No more standing in one spot staring. I'd been generous enough, having allowed her that bit of pleasure before a great amount of pain. Her time was up.

If only I'd stuck with that sentiment and pulled the trigger...

"Did you enjoy the show? You seem like the sort to enjoy such a thing. Observer of human nature."

"I did while it lasted. Unfortunately..."

"... our time is up."

"That's just it."

"Before you get all trigger happy. I know where he keeps the money."

She must have taken me for a fool. A real capital S schmuck. But it didn't matter because she was right all along—I'd been tailed. A couple of goons sent to make sure I didn't botch this up. They had a time limit, dictated by The Boss; so while I thought her time was up, it should have been up a long time ago. Now both of ours was up, and I knew this by the turning of the handle behind me. And since the writer is trying to impress his Editor with little cute references of what sunsets look like in Moncton, New Brunswick—because get this, this is where the Editor is from—still trying to perfect the opening 'enormous bay window' scene, I will have to pull double duty as narrator and exposition writer (although I already did that with a flashback scene to my failed marriage didn't I? And unlike that lazy prick I always keep exposition writing in the present tense. Screw that third person impersonal bullshit) because what followed was a close quarters shootout.

"What is it?"

"Everything and nothing at the same time."

Michael gestures for her to stay silent. Her whole being projects uneasiness. She gets up from the chair. Michael gestures again, this time for her to stand back. She huddles helplessly against the back wall. There is a clicking sound. The knob fully turns. The door bursts open. Michael aims the gun at the intruder's face, and fires twice. The intruder fires a single shot before he collapses on the floor. The bullet collides with the pillow on the bed. Alessandra frantically screams.

"It's good you decided to get out of that chair. Now get dressed."

Michael swiftly picks up the hastily removed dress lying abandoned on the floor. Without losing momentum, he throws it to the slightly stunned Alessandra. All it takes is that gesture and the look on his face for her to realize the seriousness of the situation. While she dresses, he crouches next to the corpse and turns the bloody head sideways—an ear device treacherously reveals itself. She looks at him quizzically while continuing to clothe herself.

"Familiar to you? Or are you just checking for wax?"

"He has an earpiece."

"Meaning?"

"Meaning there's a lot more of them, and we will be lucky to get out of here with our lives intact."

"Well, aren't you an optimist."

He ignores her words, walks over to the window and notices two conspicuous cars below.

"We have to move. They will move quicker once they don't hear from him."

"Can't you reply for him?" She ties the straps around her neck, securing the dress in place.

"I am not an impersonator."

She hurriedly grabs her purse from the nightstand.

"Let's hope you are the better hitman."

Michael opens the door in one fluid motion. Alessandra hides behind him. He grasps her hand firmly as he steps out into the hallway. They move unitedly, a grafted togetherness, moving toward the elevator, with both noticing upon shortening the distance, an arm's length away from the button, the elevator already steadily rising, and now looming dangerously close to their floor.

"Catering?"

He looks in the direction of the hallway.

"Take the left stairwell, and I will take the right."

His suggestion arouses a look of horror.

"You're leaving me?!"

"We stand a better chance if we separate."

"What am I supposed to do when I meet one of them?!"

He looks at her, callously. "You are a seductress. Seduce. And then shoot him in the crotch with this."

He reaches inside his jacket and retrieves a small calibre weapon. Her hands tremble as she takes the weapon from him. He turns away, and heads for the stairwell to the right. She remains immovable in her hopelessness and continues to watch him. He briefly pauses near the door, makes eye contact with her, then disappears behind it.

Once Michael enters the right stairwell and the door shuts behind him, he instantly realizes he is not alone. He hears noises. As above, so below him. He feels claustrophobically cornered. A face manifests itself from concealment of the upper stairwell directly above him, a face that's part of a whole, a body in malicious motion, with injurious intentions, a malevolent arm swings forward, hand grasps, finger squeezes... the trigger, part of a gun grasped tightly in that hand, as it releases fury, wildly uncoordinated shots springing forth and striking the walls all around Michael, but astonishingly never him directly. He never moves, standing still, remaining deadly calm, until in a perfectly reactionary manner he discharges his silenced weapon, eliminating the above threat before he backs away and turns his weapon on the threat below.

I apologize, dear readers, if this next part isn't up to par, but it did require a fair share of guess-work on my part. What may read as a false narrative is merely me grasping at straws, trying to fill in the unfilled, tell what was untold to me.

Alessandra cautiously opens the door to the left stairwell, but immediately she is grabbed and slammed hard against the wall. A barrel of a handgun gets pressed underneath her chin. She attempts to swallow but the henchman's meaty hand repositions the gun, blocking her attempt. She quickly becomes breathless, gasping for air. Michael's advice comes back to her. She gently forces the barrel of the gun down with her hand, swallows the lump in her throat and alters her usual tonal frequency, tuning it to the more alluring; the more seductive.

"If you are going to kill me, wouldn't you rather have a bit of fun with me first? Unless you prefer my corpse with those necrophiliac fetishes some men have."

He slaps her across her face. A little stream of blood runs down from the corner of her mouth.

"Forgive me. Why did I think necrophilia? You are clearly into more aristocratic fetishes, like battering women. One of those men who like to hit. Well, go ahead. Hit me some more."

He repeatedly hits her several times. She pretends to enjoy his abuse.

"I said hit me, don't slap me."

He punches her at her command. A dark

discoloration forms instantly on her cheek.

"You like that don't you, you pervert. Don't you want to kiss my sensual bloody lips?"

Alessandra stretches her pinkish-hued tongue out and enticingly licks the blood from her upper lip. He kisses her hard. They exchange saliva and blood as he gropes her chest. Her hand reaches into her purse discreetly, retrieves the small caliber weapon and fires without any second thought. She leaves the moaning, woman-battering mafioso henchman behind to bleed to death as she takes the stairs, changing stairwells along the way and finally running into Michael as he presses another henchman's face brutally into the wall and fires a single point-blank shot. Blood sprays and runs down the wall. He finally turns to her.

"You survived. Congratulations."

"You left me you bastard!"

He returns his weapon to its holster-prison under his arm.

"Watch your tone with me. I am the only person who can get you out of here alive."

He opens the door, discreetly looks about

both hallways, and leads the way to the Garbage Chute Room, pulling back the door.

"Ladies first."

"Burn in hell."

Instead of showing you the scene, would it be wrong if I made a comparison? The garbage chute symbolized a descent into something that could only equal the lowest depths. Yes, I'd say that's exactly what it symbolized. A spot-on comparison. For the more morbidly curious, sticklers for details and so on, questioning achievability and such, imagine a festering smell of rotting flesh, imagine an escalator to Dante's Inferno, imagine a noxious hot hell. Perfectly possible, but something that should be avoidable at all costs. Of course, we ended up in the basement of the building, not hell, where we stole some poor bastard's brand-new car, driving the story forward and bringing it closer to the present.

Michael grips the wheel firmly, deliberately presses down on the gas pedal, pushes the stolen vehicle to its limits. Alessandra occupies the passenger seat. She keeps touching her bloody lips. He finally notices her repetitive gestures; notices she is hurt. He takes out a handkerchief and throws it to her. *I always had a thing for throwing things to people, or at them.*

"Wipe the blood from your face. It draws too much unneeded attention."

She looks down at the handkerchief, contemplates if she should accept his brutish gesture, a momentary pause before she succumbs, wraps the handkerchief around her hand and dabs at her bloodied lip. The white handkerchief slowly soaks up the blood and turns pink. Alessandra takes it away from her face and wrings it in her hands.

"You are just afraid people might think it's your handiwork."

Michael slows the car down, timing the brake release with a brutal slap across Alessandra's face. Her lower lip splits open even more, gushing blood which fills her mouth and stains her teeth.

"What's next, you are going to bruise my bruises?"

"Open your mouth."

He forces it open for her. One hand pries her

mouth open while the other shoves the barrel of his gun inside. Her body violently jerks as the weapon slithers down her throat.

"You see, we have a little problem. I think you are withholding something. Actually, 'I think' isn't the right phrase. I know you are withholding something from me."

Alessandra attempts to speak. The gun prevents her from doing just that. She really tries to speak, but she just spews bloody saliva and incomprehensibilities. Tears start to run down her face. Michael watches her, unmoved by the sight. She sheds more tears. Tears that follow in the tracks of their predecessors. He finally removes the gun from her mouth. The barrel is coated with sticky saliva and traces of red lipstick. She breaks out into a raging cough. He pays her no mind and wipes the gun clean on his pant leg. She finally regains control of herself and turns to him. Their eyes meet.

"Do you hate me now?"

"Hate? No, I despise you."

Alessandra gives Michael a look, a mix of arousal and hatred. He reciprocates. Lust overtakes them. He forces her toward him. His lips entwine with hers. She half-heartedly fights him off, then swiftly surrenders to her overwhelming urge. A few minutes of pure animal passion, and it is all over. All that built up frustration satisfied; their desire disperses like the carbon monoxide from the stolen vehicle's tailpipe. They sit back down in their seats. Both breathe hard and try their best to arrange their clothes, make themselves presentable again. He takes a pack of cigarettes from his jacket pocket, retrieves a single smoke and lights it. She turns the front-view mirror toward herself, takes out a red lipstick from her purse and carefully traces her lips with it.

"How much does he have in the safe?"

"Enough."

"Never is there such a thing as enough when you are dealing with people like us. Our hearts pump greed faster than blood."

He stares ahead, through the windshield

and past it, absorbed, lost in thought, trying to detect mobility in the wintry wasteland ahead. She watches him with unconcealed hunger, waiting for his mystification to wear off, feeling the pangs, experiencing full on parasitic uncontrollable itching for capital. He empties his mouth from the latest drag's chemical contents before turning to her, his mind set on something concrete.

"Either we run, or we try to get this money."

This is how you create tension and write a realistic scene. But here comes the hack, defeated and tired of redrafting his 'enormous bay window' scene. He is cheating. Jumping ahead in the narrative. Working on the scene I just shared with you. Let's hear his god awful politically-correct version of the same events.

Michael drives. Alessandra occupies the passenger seat, next to him but oblivious to his state of mind, worrying herself with her own worrisome thoughts, all the while touching her bloodied lip repeatedly and obsessively. Both are silent. The tension inside the car constricts them, driver and passenger, nervousness replacing talkativeness. Suddenly, her words pierce through the established vocal immobility, secured by mutual agreement, mutual silence, cutting through the human noiselessness inside the vehicle.

"You are just going to drive all night without uttering a word?"

"Talking ruins things. You talked and now look where it's gotten us."

"You are the one who decided to listen."

"I did. Like an idiot, meddling in a private affair that did not concern me."

"Well, now that you have me all to yourself, I am honestly surprised you wouldn't want to pull over at once and force yourself on me for all the trouble I've caused you."

"You'd like that, wouldn't you? You live for this drama. Probably find it exciting?"

"I enjoy turning heads. Commanding a room full of dapper men with hungry eyes and wide-open mouths dribbling at the sight of me. I like to flirt. I like to tease. Even the occasional striptease behind closed doors. What I don't particularly enjoy is being splattered with blood and viscera, or you know, being shot at. To each their own, I suppose. These are just not my kinks. But it could be worse."

"How is that?"

"We could be dead, or one of them could be alive to report back. The way I figure it, whether you've caught on or not, you have been driving to his house all this time. Subconsciously, you took in what I said about the money. We still have time. A small amount. Just enough to use to our advantage."

He didn't do too bad, actually. He even changed it to the present, erroneously forgetting he started off in past tense. I honestly expected worse. Now he is all exhausted, clamoring for a break, mentally worn out from writing down a few sentences. Typical. One of those writers who hold themselves up to unrealistic standards. Expecting to wrench brilliancy from every goddamn sentence. Let him take his undeserved break while we continue.

"Run where? You can't be this naïve. He will find us. If that's your plan you might as well pull over right now, take out your gun and blow your brains out. I will use it right after you."

"Sure you would."

"You don't trust me?"

"I don't trust anyone. Especially some broad."

"I could be your broad."

"If we get the money."

"If we get that money."

"You have it all planned out. Don't you?"

"Always have to have a plan. We are all out here looking for something. Figure out what it is and draft up a plan of how you are going to get it."

"That simple."

"That simple."

"Why'd'you do that, anyway? Behind his back."

"He's been around the block. And so have I. His kindness wasn't limitless. Sure, our relationship afforded me a certain lavish lifestyle. He constantly gave me money and never showed up empty-handed. But I wasn't the wife. I was the girl on the side. I like the security of knowing where I will wake up the next day without dependence on someone who might one day trade me in for a younger tart with a higher breast-line and pointier nipples. Until he came along, I didn't have any security, and I knew I never wanted to experience that again in case he tried to take it away. So, I sought and scavenged, always keeping my eyes out for an opportunity, much like the one fallen into our laps. I don't know about you, but I am tired of relying on others. I want to set myself up for the future."

"You want the perks without him around. And what makes me so different?"

"The money would be split equally, no obligations; if it works it works. And if it doesn't, we can move on. Go our separate ways financially secure."

"You are a natural deceiver. I don't know what to believe. I look at you and all I see is a facade. The revealing clothes you wear, your dyed hair, saucy demeanor, those large saucer eyes with the overload of makeup. You stand out. You want to stand out. But that's not you. That's not who you are. It's all an illusion, attempt to change your whole persona."

She fixes her stare out the passenger-side window. "Haven't you ever wanted to live your life as someone else? Just start over again?"

"I just haven't met anyone who went to all this trouble to get it."

"Then you never met anyone who wanted it enough."

"Alright, you got yourself a partner. But we won't be sharing a bed."

"You sure about that?"

"I can't sleep with anyone beside me."

"A man who likes his sleep. I can respect that."

I didn't tell her right then and there that I wanted to be someone else as well. She would have laughed and told me to write us out of this mess. She was the real writer. She had it all down pat. And she was right. Some people just don't want it enough. I didn't. Otherwise, I would have never gotten in this hole. Writers write, the Ukrainian Canadian prick writing this story is writing, failing, sure, but he is trying, you can tell he wants it, to be up there with the greats. Tried more than I did, anyway. I just fell prey to my unstable mind and piling rejection letters.

Michael pulls the car over. Keeps out of sight of the large mansion ahead.

"You will find him alone, waiting for his men to return. Don't underestimate him. Many others have, and none are around to boast about it. *Remember.* He keeps everything in the safe inside of his office. You will need the combination... unless you also moonlight as a safecracker when not living your dream job of a trigger man. With a man like this, I wouldn't rule out torture, he isn't one to blabber on and on without some prodding."

A woman without limits. I was just as surprised as you are now, dear voracious readers/bookworms (burrowing deeper into the book, tunneling through the printed text, hanging onto every word) that she didn't carry around a pair of pliers in her purse for the job of teeth pulling, you know if torture shall arise, as it clearly has now. Alas, it was too late to brake, to break away. She had me where she wanted me, won over and enticed. I'd never be able to stay out of trouble with her around. It followed her wherever she went. And now she recruited me to disburse pain, collect money, nominal sympathy for the poor sucker about to get tortured and murdered. Murder was obligatory in a situation like this. Something I would not be able to avoid. I knew it as soon as I stepped out of the car. Desperate people in desperate situations with grim prospects, unless they commit to carrying out desperate deeds in hopes of large rewards.

"Do you know how I knew you wanted the money?"

"Shoot."

"I thought that was your job."

"Smartass."

"When I first brought it up, and you didn't give me that uninterested look."

"So, it was my eyes that gave me away."

"Forget about your eyes. Come here. Come, give me a kiss."

"I love kissing wrong women, leading me toward a world of danger."

"Here."

She reaches inside her purse, perusing the interior until she has what she needs, a candy cane. She takes it out, her fingers waste no time unwrapping it. She inserts it in her slightly ajar mouth and starts to reduce the diameter down with her moist tongue, all wholesomeness withdrawn, lascivious behavior on full display for Michael's sole benefit. A spectator resuming his seat. When she has it exactly the way she wants it, she hands it back, thinned down on one end, made razor sharp by her luscious lips and tongue.

"For luck."

Inside the car, they talk, collaboratively, have a conspiratorial conversation, confer about things until both reach agreement exchanging nods before Michael gladly steps out of the smoke-filled crammed space greedily gobbling up fresh outdoor air—all this land, seemingly offering up widening opportunities, while the mind, the mental abacus that it is, rejects aesthetic pleasure and refrains from making painfully obvious observations, instead: zeroing in and narrowing probabilities until only one sure path remains. He turns to her. She smiles the eager smile of the unemployed and desperate, incisors on full display, life-sharpened, nicotine and coffee-stained sickly yellowed teeth from all the long days and late nights of plotting and scheming, momentarily caught by moonlight. Michael turns away, starts on foot toward the mansion in the distance, proprietor of a preoccupied mind, necessity for cash nipping him all over. Money, the stipulation for happiness. Her voice ringing in his ears, attuned to her serpentine words, nearing the mansion now, the big score, a simply irresistible opportunity to a pair of parasitic individuals.

Wouldn't you know it? I think I imitated the pretentious bastard perfectly there. My gritty realism with his fanciful wordplay and melodramatic touches for the daytime soap opera crowd. Soon you won't be able to tell us apart. The corpse as you have probably guessed by now is of my ex-Boss. And believe me when I say he was one tough bastard. This wasn't some snotty teenager, this was a seasoned pro. Weathered, sure, but still with a few tricks up his sleeve. I hurled myself at him; he met me head-on, engaged me in an animalistic ritual. It was a beautiful sort of brutalization, a bewildering display of cruelty, a pair of uncaged snarling mongrels constantly colliding, gripping and grappling, wildly throwing punches, trying to land that fatal punch, smashing into furniture, their

*bodies suffering, tortured, driven to the limits with
no time to recover, to catch their breath, swinging
and being swung on, fists hammering, mouths
spewing saliva and profanities, faces becoming
bloodier and bloodier and then a hand reaching,
inconspicuously procuring a candy cane of all
things, and with one swift movement the unsheathed
treat becomes a weapon, thrusting through the
eyeball and reaching the brain, a spike piercing and
penetrating, resulting in immediate brain death.
And there you have it, folks: a description of how
the once mighty fall from grace. A mafioso version
of Julius Caesar done in with a candy cane. And
here I am now, sitting on this crate waiting for my
better half, partner in crime, and something tells
me I won't have to wait long. Just a heads up, have
some patience folks, narrating in real time will be
a challenge, now that we are all caught up, with
the hard part out of the way, done away with the
murder and all and at last synched up to the present
time. But if you learned anything about me, is that
I am always up for a challenge.*

The cellar stairs squeak. Swift footsteps approach. Thunderbolt strikes. High heels on the stairs. Michael takes a last puff on his cigarette. He throws it down and crushes it with his scuffed leather shoe before he puts both of his hands inside his pants' pockets. Alessandra appears from the shadows, looking the part, the definition of desirability and eroticism. Her eyes pause on the dead body. Michael does not register shock or surprise in that impersonal gaze, just the absence of emotion.

"He was an obnoxious prick, but he seemed to know my pleasure points. Think you can figure them out by yourself? Don't think you can ask him now."

She moves closer, within reach. He touches her. She allows the touch, allows him to proceed. His hand on her leg, a hand constantly in motion. She responds, shuddering with pleasure, crumbling at the correctness of his touch.

"Warmer. Now go higher."

He moves his hand higher along her thigh. She gasps in ecstasy.

"Are you actually enjoying this, or have you consciously programmed yourself to like this?"

She banishes his hand from her thigh.

"Does this feel fake to you?"

She pushes him down. Straddles him. Floats above him, lost in her own erotic abandonment. He submits to her. Indulges. Admires her non-prudishness as she bares it all. An equestrian in her saddle. Two bodies in unified motion.

"Never figured you for the submissive sort," she says.

"You went to all this trouble. I might as well let you indulge. We can always switch later."

She bites his neck, breaks the skin, draws blood. They groan simultaneously. Clutch one another. Suffocate in their tightness. Magnets stuck together. He glides his hands across her drenched body. It glistens with sweat. Her sweat coats his hands. They both give themselves over, pursue their pleasures, satisfy their cravings.

"Did you get it?"

"What do you think?"

"I think you'd be a complete fool to have murdered him without getting that combination."

"The bag is right over there..." He nods in the direction of the bag. Her eyes follow his directional nod. The bag sits equidistant from the crate with his jacket and gun left on top and her purse thrown on the floor in the moment of heat next to a woodworking table.

"Full?"

"It's full. There's only one problem."

"There's not enough in there for two."

"There isn't."

"Which only means..."

"...which only means that only one of us is walking out of here alive."

She breaks away, sprints toward her purse, starts to fiendishly search inside. Michael cocks the gun. The sound startles her, makes her stop her frenzied search.

"I never carry just one gun. Don't you

remember from the hotel? A small caliber weapon fits a pants pocket just as well as a jacket without drawing any attention to itself. Always assume a man with a second gun has a third." He pulls his pants up. "Lay the gun down."

She retrieves Michael's other small caliber weapon from her purse and reluctantly lays it down on a table next to her.

"You are beautiful but sadly conniving to the point where trust is out of the question."

"You are the one with the gun. I am unarmed. Naked. There's little to fear."

"I fear the gossip. A witness to a murder talking to law enforcement in the near future. That mouth of yours tends to flap uncontrollably."

"Well, make it stop, lover. Give it a kiss."

Michael decides to take her up on her proposition. He raises his gun, aims it directly at her chest, walks over and kisses her passionately.

"God, you are beautiful."

"Obviously not beautiful enough for you to keep alive."

"Sadly, no."

Aghhhhhh…

[Shut up! You are ruining the scene with your agonizing screaming. The audience needs to know what happened.]

Alessandra reaches toward the nape of her neck, retrieving a taped down replacement razor blade, concealed by her long lustrous hair. Straightaway she slashes through the air and Michael's neck. He loses his balance, stumbles around, clutching at his throat, unable to stop the bleeding, dripping blood all over the floor, resisting against death's encroachment. She watches him, unaffected by his suffering. He sits down on the crate to keep from falling, ending the mad dashing about the space. The restlessness is now only inside of his mind, the restlessness of a man nearing his end.

"Isn't your darling absolutely deplorable? You must despise her. Coaxing you into a trap like that. Do you want a handkerchief? You are gushing all over your recently procured, former employer's spotless starched-white dress shirt. Or how about a glass of cold water? Something to help clear that lump in your throat."

Her savage snickering fills the cellar. She picks his jacket up from the crate, reaches inside, takes out a crumpled pack of cigarettes and lights one up. He continues to bleed profusely. She takes a long draw on his cigarette, blows out a few smoke rings toward his face, the rings expanding until they dissolve upon facial impact, adding another layer of pain to his contorted face.

"Men and their inability to turn down any form of sex." She shakes her head. "I spread my legs and here comes my knight in shinning armor. I offer a kiss and here he is again, galloping at full speed with a hard on instead of a lance or a sword, wanting to play his little power games and exchange saliva, bacteria and mucus. How pathetic and sad. Don't you understand your current predicament was foreseeable. You just didn't look hard enough, didn't pay close enough attention to the warning signs. You aren't cut out for this. That's the bottom line. The stakes are higher, there are no second prizes for the runners-up. You don't get your little ribbon. You are lucky if you walk away with your life. And clearly, you haven't been that lucky. Self-control and a bit of street smarts is all it takes to navigate this shapeless world. Slapping women and pointing guns will only get you so far. You should have known better. You should have learned along the way. Got to know yourself a bit better. Understood who you were and where you belonged. I understood the moment I saw you. I can always tell a mark a mile away."

Alessandra picks up the bag. Halfway up the stairs, she shuts the lights on the doubled over prisoner, plunging him with a single switch, a single brushstroke into black bituminous all eclipsing darkness. And she is gone. The red-haired, scheming temptress from hell. What attracted Michael to her, attracted many men in his position now. She would have got you too, dear reader. Her strength. Her intelligence. Her sexual allure. You are in denial if you are under the impression she could ever love anyone except herself. Ruthless and deadly. Temptress par excellence.

I didn't see this coming.

[But I did.]

Oh, it's you, you sniveling bastard. You have discovered my additions, followed the trail of my internal thoughts.

[I did. That is why I am letting you bleed out now. You could have had the money. But you got greedy. Backstabbing. This is punishment for your tempering.]

I hate your ending.

[Of course, you do. I am sure you had a better one planned.]

After I had gotten the money and killed that long-legged bimbo, I would have driven away with one last thought on my mind. A flashback scene that repeats itself constantly in my life. Reminding me not to forget it, to let it slip away. A scene I always questioned. Taking place during my drunkard days. Fittingly, a scene that supposedly happened in a bar.

[I know the one you are talking about. It's on the cutting-room floor.]

You bastard! It would have been perfect.

[Possibly, but we'll never know now.]

Do me a favor. Type it out just for me. For my eyes only. The reader doesn't have to see it. I know I messed up, that's just who I am, a fuck-up. Grant a dying man his dying wish—I will be eternally grateful.

[What does it matter now. Have it your way. I'll even do it in your style.]

Mix our styles.

Michael enters a Sin City pavilion attached to the main building. A member-only joint. A place where you can freely move around without worrying about law enforcement and scores that need to be settled in a public place—mob enforcers following the ordinance of the higher ups, sending their calling-card murder messages.

He takes a seat at the counter, striking in his expensive new suit. The bartender nods. He knows Michael, many others do as well. A glass of whisky magically appears before him, sparkling invitingly under all the lights. Before he has time to raise it to his thirsty lips, he feels a hand on his shoulder. Michael turns, suddenly face to face with his scantily dressed ex-wife, hardly recognisable behind all the caked-on makeup and the large serving tray in her hands. She uncertainly looks him over.

"Michael?"

"Last time I checked."

"Not exactly what I hoped you would say."

"You work here?"

"I do."

"Well, you should know better than to talk about hope. Hope comes here to die." He could tell she felt the brunt of his condescending tone. "Looks like a reversal of fortune from where I am sitting."

"Spiteful. You've probably been waiting for this day for a long while now. So, go on you fucker, rub it in."

He looks over her shoulder: a gentleman at the end of the bar is attempting to get her attention. "We will have to continue this some other time. You got a customer to service."

Her complexion becomes frighteningly pale. He finishes his drink in one gulp, standing up, a self-satisfying smile playing across his lips. With his back to the only woman he ever loved, the self-proclaimed victor walks away.

Did this really happen? Did I really hurt her a second time around? Threw away my only chance for redemption? For happiness?

[I don't know. Only you would know the answer to this. All I know is that you have never walked away 'victoriously' from anything in your life. And now its time for you to die and for me to type The End, concluding this cautionary tale which should make the readers feel better about their own lives, those nice and boring and very safe lives.]

ABOUT THE AUTHOR

A native of Kyiv, Ukraine, but living in Canada since the age of eleven, Nick Voro discovered literature at an early age, never quite mustering the ability to put an excellent book down. A recent graduate of the Toronto Film School, Nick divides his time between being a full-time parent and a full-time author.

His debut work, *Conversational Therapy: Stories and Plays*, has recently sold over 200 copies and is part of the library system (United States, Canada, New Zealand, Australia and Scotland).

Lee D. Thompson, an editor and writer from Moncton, New Brunswick, Canada, edited this short story. His books include: a novel in [xxx] dreams from Broken Jaw Press, Mouth Human Must Die from Frog Hollow Press and Apastoral: A Mistopia from Corona/Samizdat. His short fiction has been published in many anthologies, including Random House's Victory Meat, New Fiction from Atlantic Canada and Vagrant Press's The Vagrant Revue of New Fiction. He is the winner of the David Adams Richards Prize (2018) and New Brunswick Book Award (2022). He is the publisher of Galleon Books.

9 781738 319954